928 9

Ashley,

Mary Christine
to George Wilson

Christmas Always...

Story and paintings by
Peter Catalanotto

ORCHARD BOOKS   NEW YORK

For Chelsea, the sweetest gift of all

Thanks to Jim, Joyce, Caroline, Katie, and especially my father

Orchard Books, A division of Franklin Watts, Inc., 387 Park Avenue South, New York, NY 10016

Manufactured in the United States of America. Printed by General Offset Company, Inc.
Bound by Horowitz/Rae. Book design by Mina Greenstein.

The text of this book is set in 16 point ITC Zapf International Medium. The illustrations are
watercolor paintings reproduced in full color.   10   9   8   7   6   5   4   3   2   1

Library of Congress Cataloging-in-Publication Data
Catalanotto, Peter. Christmas always— / story and paintings by Peter Catalanotto.   p.   cm.
Summary: At bedtime on Christmas Eve, Katie is visited by the Sandman, Jack Frost, and the
Tooth Fairy, all of whom hastily leave when they hear the arrival of the most important visitor of all.
ISBN 0-531-05946-4.   ISBN 0-531-08546-5 (lib. bdg.)
[1. Christmas—Fiction. 2. Bedtime—Fiction.] I. Title. PZ7.C26878Ch 1991 90-28712

Bedtime always comes too early . . .

. . . especially on Christmas Eve.

"Good-night, Katie dear," said Mother.
Father smiled, saying, "Sleep tight."
Grandma said, "Sweet dreams, lambie,"
as she kissed her for everybody.
Then Grandpa, chuckling, took Katie up to bed.

"See my loose tooth, Grandpa?" she asked.
"Good for you, honey. Now, brush carefully and I'll read to you."

" 'Happy Christmas to all,' " the book ended,
" 'and to all a good night.' "

"Grandpa, I never get to stay up with everyone."
"Never say never," he said. "Besides, Katie, you need
 to be asleep when *he* comes."
"Who, Grandpa?"
"You know who. Now, cuddle down. Good-night, little one."

Alone in her room, Katie listened to the grown-ups
talking downstairs.
I'll never fall asleep, she thought, wiggling her tooth

when—oops—

the tooth popped out and fell to the floor.
Katie bent to look for it, and was startled to see—
a tiny man staring back at her.
"Who are you?" she asked.

"You know who I am," he said in a small, gravelly voice.
"I always come at night, when it's time for you to sleep."
"The Sandman!" Katie whispered, amazed.
She felt herself lifted magically from the bed,
then tucked again beneath the covers.

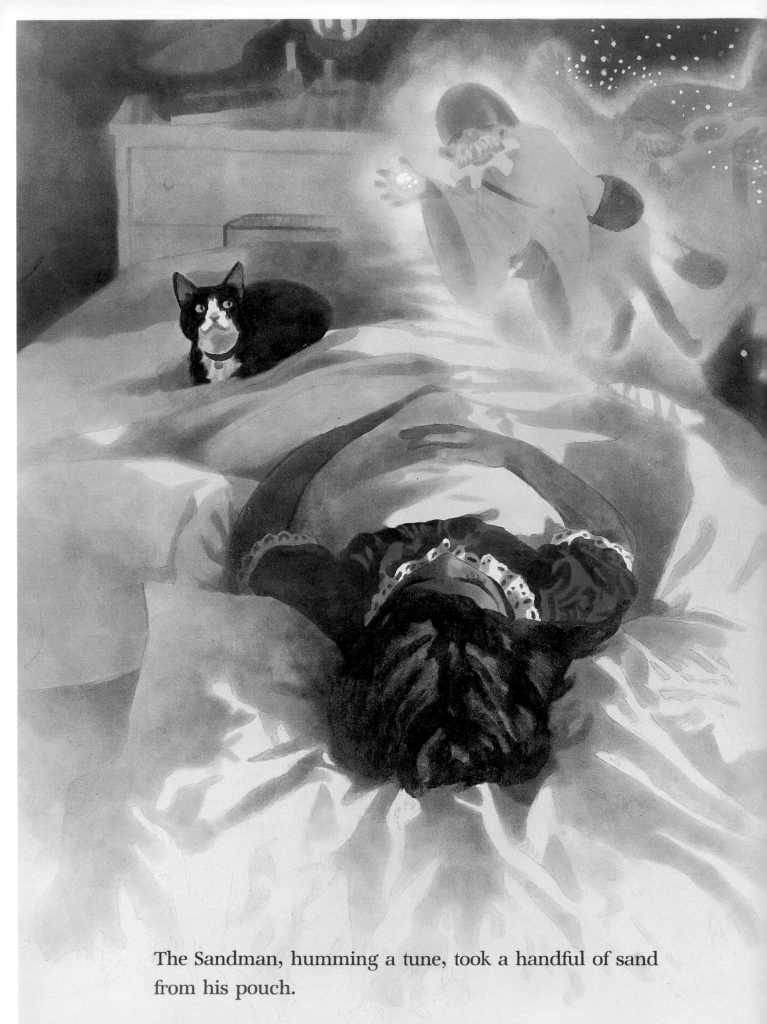

The Sandman, humming a tune, took a handful of sand from his pouch.

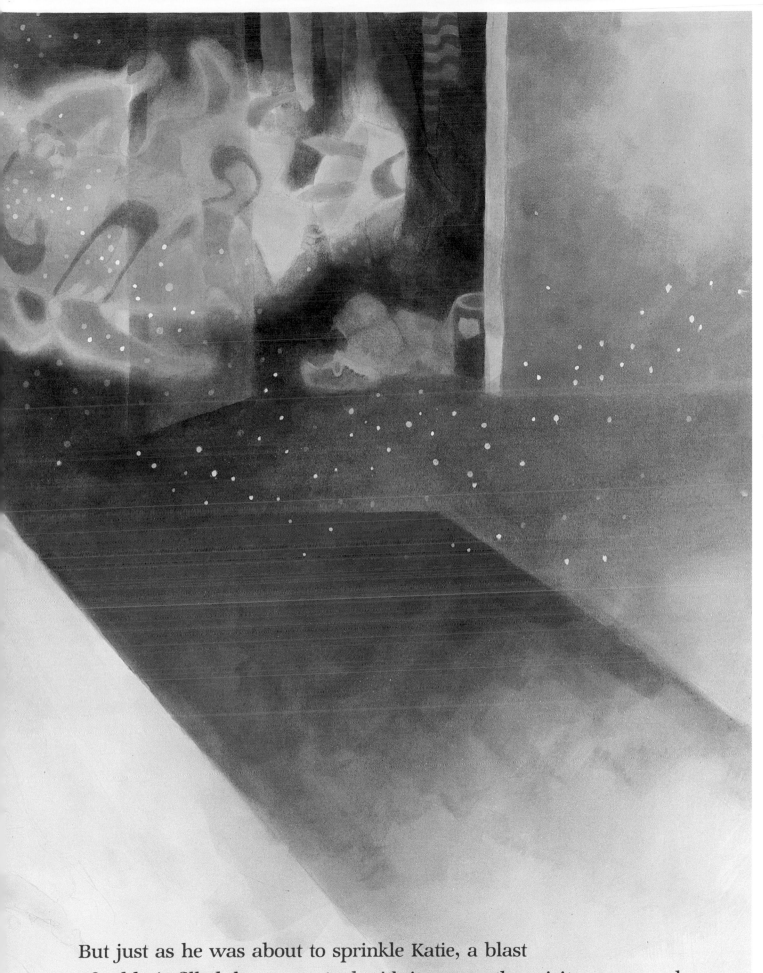

But just as he was about to sprinkle Katie, a blast
of cold air filled the room. And with it . . . another visitor appeared.

"Who are you?" Katie asked.
"You know who I am," he said. "I always come in winter,
  to make sure it's cold for Christmas."
"Jack Frost!" Katie cried, absolutely astonished.

"That's all fine and dandy, Jack," sputtered the Sandman,
"but you just spoiled one of my finest sleep spells."
  With a *crrraaaccck* he snapped an icicle
  off Jack Frost's nose.
"Oocha-ma-goocha!" Jack cried, shooting into the air.
  The next moment, the Sandman was hopping and hollering,
  a shower of snow down his back.

"*SSSSHHHH!*" Katie cried at the two of them.
"Everyone will hear us!"
A shimmer of light spun into the room—and on it danced . . .
yet another visitor.

"Who are you?" Katie asked.

"You know who I am," she twittered. "I always come
   when you lose a tooth. But it's not under your pillow, child."

"Ummm . . ." said Katie. "I . . . think it's under the bed,
   Tooth Fairy."

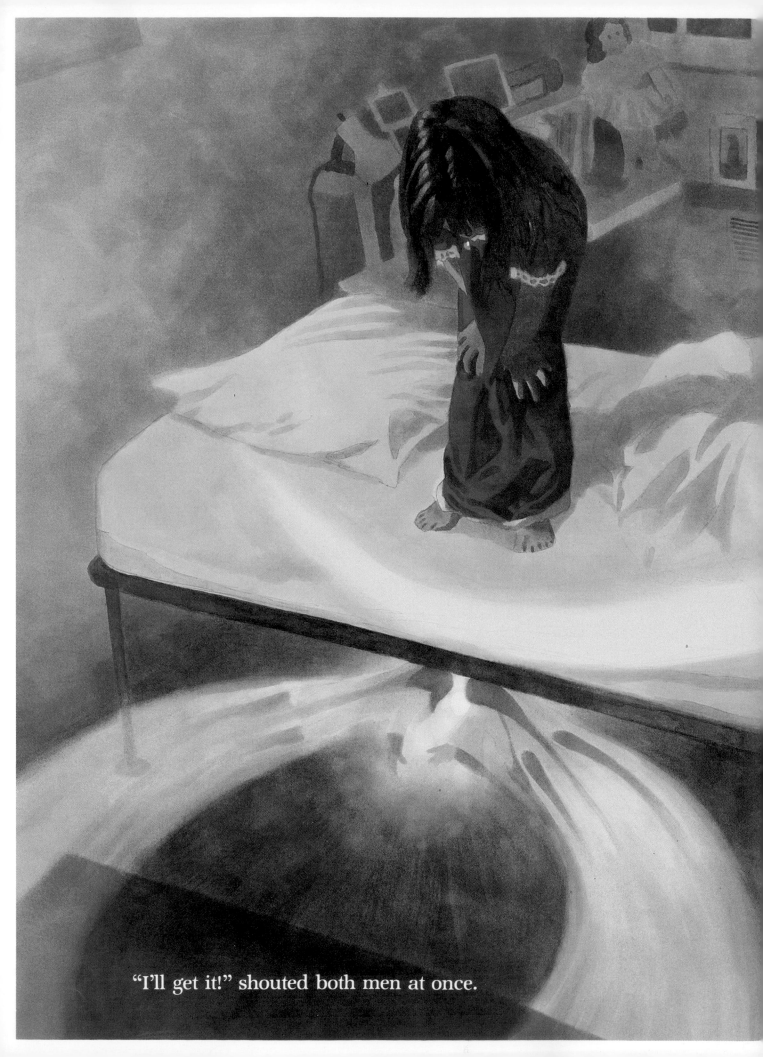

"I'll get it!" shouted both men at once.

"Oh, my!" the Tooth Fairy gasped. "You two! And *still* here! You *know* what night this is. You know who's coming! Please . . . finish your work and be off!"

"Indeed!" said Jack Frost. "Watch this, Katie."

"And now this," the Sandman began . . .
when suddenly, the sound of footsteps could be heard
on the stairs—

footsteps . . . and brightly jingling bells.
"Here he comes!" Katie cried. "And none of us are in bed!"
"Here he comes," said the Tooth Fairy, disappearing
as she blew Katie a kiss.

"Here he comes!" said Jack Frost, and with a quick bow
he sped out the window.

"Here he comes!" said the Sandman, sprinkling Katie with sand,
and, in a whirlwind, vanishing.
Katie yawned. "He's here, but now I'll never get
to see him. . . ."

Softly, the night's final visitor crossed the room.
He bent close to Katie's cheek, whispering,
"Never say never."

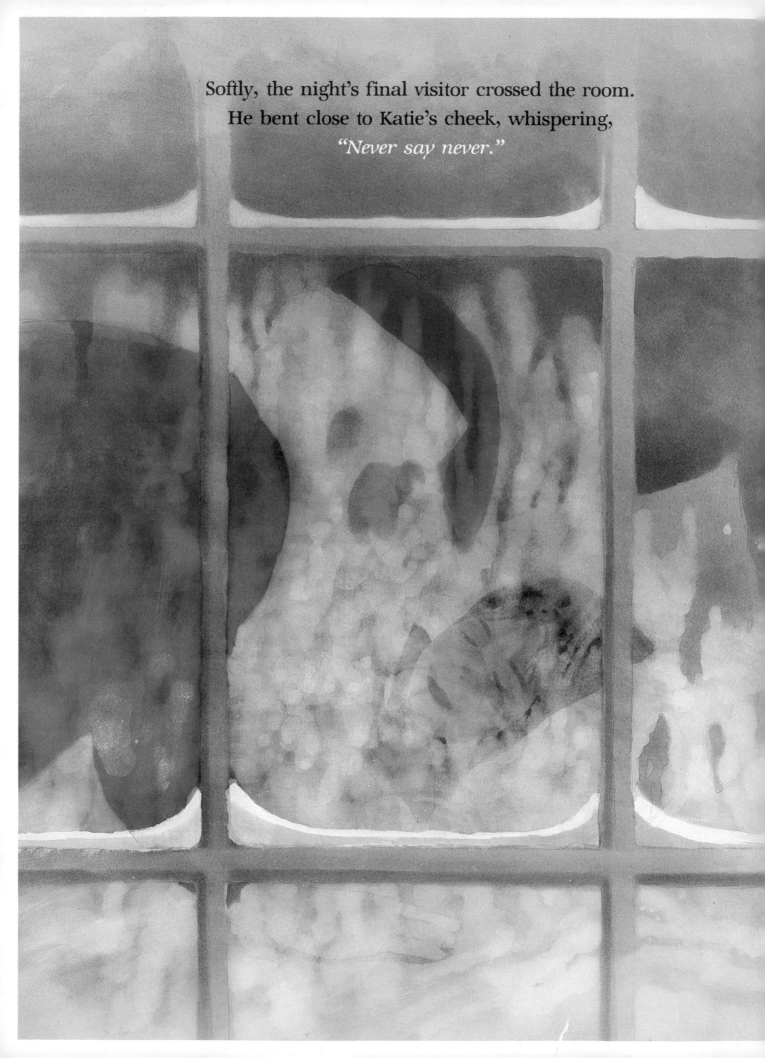